P9-EAJ-184

Also by Patricia MacLachlan

Dream Within a Dream

WITHDRAWN

Dream Within a Dream

Patricia MacLachlan

Margaret K. McElderry Books
New York   London   Toronto   Sydney   New Delhi

MARGARET K. McELDERRY BOOKS
An imprint of Simon & Schuster Children's Publishing Division
1230 Avenue of the Americas, New York, New York 10020
This book is a work of fiction. Any references to historical events, real people, or real places are used fictitiously. Other names, characters, places, and events are products of the author's imagination, and any resemblance to actual events or places or persons, living or dead, is entirely coincidental.
Text copyright © 2019 by Patricia MacLachlan
Jacket illustration copyright © 2019 by Amy June Bates
All rights reserved, including the right of reproduction in whole or in part in any form.
MARGARET K. McELDERRY BOOKS is a trademark of Simon & Schuster, Inc.
For information about special discounts for bulk purchases, please contact Simon & Schuster Special Sales at 1-866-506-1949 or business@simonandschuster.com.
The Simon & Schuster Speakers Bureau can bring authors to your live event. For more information or to book an event, contact the Simon & Schuster Speakers Bureau at 1-866-248-3049 or visit our website at www.simonspeakers.com.
Book design by Debra Sfetsios-Conover
The text for this book was set in Baskerville MT.
Manufactured in the United States of America
0419 FFG
First Edition
2 4 6 8 10 9 7 5 3 1
Library of Congress Cataloging-in-Publication Data
Names: MacLachlan, Patricia.
Title: Dream within a dream / Patricia MacLachlan.
Description: First edition. | New York : Margaret K. McElderry Books, [2019] | Summary: Eleven-year-old aspiring writer Louisa considers traveling the world with her globetrotting parents, but friendship with George helps her to see her grandparents' farm on Deer Island in a new light.
Identifiers: LCCN 2018042908 (print) | ISBN 9781534429598 (hardback) | ISBN 9781534429611 (eBook)
Subjects: | CYAC: Friendship—Fiction. | Family life—Fiction. | Farm life—Fiction. | Islands—Fiction. | BISAC: JUVENILE FICTION / Family / Multigenerational. | JUVENILE FICTION / Social Issues / Adolescence. | JUVENILE FICTION / Social Issues / Friendship.
Classification: LCC PZ7.M2225 Dre 2019 (print) | DDC [Fic]—dc23
LC record available at https://lccn.loc.gov/2018042908

For my children—and their children—
with thanks to George Munemo,
who thought I should write this book.

Is *all* that we see or seem
But a dream within a dream?

—EDGAR ALLAN POE

⟋

The only thing worse than being blind is
having sight but no vision.

—HELEN KELLER

⟋

Nakupenda

—SWAHILI WORD FOR "I LOVE YOU"

Prologue

My grandfather Jake's Deer Island farm runs down to the sea—sweet grass slipping to water.

Sometimes seals sun on the warm sand.

There used to be a large flock of sheep in the field that the townspeople would help shear twice a year. Now there are only three sheep—Jake's favorites: Bitty and Flossie and Flip.

Other things have changed.

My grandfather is losing his eyesight.

He can still take care of his three sheep.

He can still cook.

He can read when he uses a large viewing machine.

But soon—the worst thing of all—is that he may not be

able to drive his beloved 1938 midnight-black Cord car with running boards.

He has proudly driven my grandmother to town for years when she doesn't walk or bicycle to the store.

He has driven his colorfully decorated car in parades and on the Fourth of July.

He has washed and polished the car.

He has loved the car.

Things are changing.

I hate change.

1

Change

I'm telling my own story here.

I'm a secret writer. My teacher has never read my journal. My mother and father have not read it either. I think my brother, Theo, has read it, but he hasn't said so. My life is like a dream within a dream, as Edgar Allan Poe writes.

For one thing my name is Louisiana. My parents were bird-watching through the South when my mother was very pregnant. What were they thinking?

So I was born in Louisiana.

My name is Louisiana. Louisa for short.

And I have a large mass of long curly red hair. Where did *that* come from?

My friends have smooth long hair that moves. My hair is long and wildly curly like an out-of-control Brillo pad. Look it up if you don't know what that is. A so-called friend once said, "Too bad about your hair, Louisa."

I am filled with anguish.

My younger brother, Theo, tells me most times boys don't bother saying rude things about hair.

Theo is strangely understanding, yet direct.

"Tough to be you, Lou," he says with sympathy when I complain to him.

"Theo is a linear thinker," says Jake. "Put words to what you are feeling and you can solve it. Like me."

Theo is only eight but could be seventy.

My grandmother Boots says the same thing in her own way.

"Theo is old," she says.

My grandmother's real name is Lily, but she is called Boots because she loves them. Everyone in her family has always worn boots, her grandmother and grandfather, her aunts and uncles and cousins everywhere. Even the babies wear boots. My favorite uncle, whose name I forget, is called Boots too. He's a poet who fell in love with cows and is now a farmer.

My grandmother Boots prefers wellies. She has four pairs in the front closet: red, green, yellow, and black. They are tall and come up to her knees.

When Uncle Boots visited, it was confusing. We tried to change my grandmother's name to Boo.

"No," she said.

"What about Wellie?"

"Never."

So now we have more than one Boots.

Boots knows most everything.

She knows, for instance, that her son—my father—and his wife—my mother—are "dense" about some things even though they're "disturbingly" intelligent, as she puts it.

Boots is my hero.

Our parents have plunked Theo and me on the little island for the long summer, as they always do, while they go off to do their bird research. My father is an ornithologist, and my mother is a photographer. You haven't seen anyone more excited than my father over the possible sighting of an ivory-billed woodpecker in some bug-ridden habitat. Or New Caledonian crows, who sometimes make and use tools to catch grubs. My mother often climbs trees to photograph a bird's nest made of animal fur, human hair, sticks, small bones, and an every-once-in-a-while treasure such as a gold bead. Sometimes baby birds in a nest squawk at her when she surprises them.

Theo refers to our parents' summers as "bird bedlam."

My father, of course, wears boots.

Theo and I love coming to Deer Island for peace, reading books, taking long walks by the water, swimming, and mostly talking to Jake and Boots. Theo talks all year long about the island as if it is his dream.

"Boots?"

"Yes?"

"I heard something when my parents were talking."

Boots nods. She is not shocked that I was eavesdropping. Nothing much shocks Boots.

"They were saying that you and Jake might move to our house when he can't see well enough to drive."

Boots laughs. Right out loud. "No. This is our home. The place we love. We can walk to almost everyplace we want to be."

"Or, they said, maybe we could move here to help," I say.

"Taking you out of school and all you know?

Don't worry, Louisa. They're not invited."

I nod, relieved. "I hate change," I say.

"Well, sometimes change *can* be exciting. An adventure. Sometimes you find out who you are."

"I don't think so," I say.

"I know so," says Boots. "Trust me. I know everything."

She puts her arms around me. "It's hard being you," she says.

"That's what Theo said!" I say.

"Of course he did," says Boots, making me laugh and cry at the same time.

Tess jumps up on us as we stand there in the kitchen.

So Boots puts on her yellow wellies, and we take Tess walking down the field, past the sheep. Tess practices her old habit of herding, nipping at their heels.

They stare and look away again, bored.

Seals are sleeping in the sun. Tess goes over, and they hiss at her. Tess prances and dances around them. She isn't afraid.

The seals aren't afraid either.

The waves are slow and calm.

"There will be a nice sunset tonight," says Boots.

"Change, Louisa. The sunset comes, then darkness comes and the moon rises, and then in the morning, the sun. Change comes, and sometimes you can't do anything about it."

"I can try," I say.

"Then you will be unhappy," says Boots.

Herring gulls fly over us, making their laughing sound.

"Jake's not unhappy," I say.

"Jake's positive. He loves his life. 'It is what it is,' he says. 'No problem,'" says Boots.

"What about if he can't drive his car?" I ask.

Boots sighs and throws a stick down the beach for Tess.

"*That* may be a small problem for him," she says flatly.

Tess runs back and drops the stick at Boots's feet. Boots throws it again.

"But something will happen," she says.

"What do you mean?"

"Something," repeats Boots. "Remember the sunset, the moon, sunrise, the morning sun. Something always happens."

The seals slip back into the sea. Tess watches them

swim off in the water. They swim on their backs and look at her. Then they dip down and are gone.

Behind them the small morning ferry leaves the island to go to the mainland. I shade my eyes and look over to the blurry mainland where I live.

But as it turns out, Boots is right.

Things do happen.

And one surprise.

I meet George.

2

Even Steven

So here is the next day of my life. I get up early. No Theo. But of course this is *my* story. Theo brings his heavy bag of books to read, always fearful that the small island library will not have the books he wants.

Theo is the watcher and listener of *my* story.

Jake is in the kitchen with Tess. He has lots of toast on the counter and is making his famous poached eggs in his six-cup poached egg pan. He tosses bits of toast over his head every so often for Tess. She runs and scrambles and jumps to catch the pieces.

He does this every morning "for her exercise," as he puts it with a smile.

Actually, it is *Jake's* exercise.

Jake looks sideways at me. He pushes a plate of toast on the counter—waiting for the egg that will sit on it.

"What are you doing this morning?" he asks.

He has a sly look to him.

He tosses a piece of toast over his head, and I reach over, catch it, and give it to Tess.

"Nothing," I say to Jake. "You have something exciting planned? Right?"

"Yep, I do."

He slips a perfectly poached egg onto my toast.

"I know that because we're kindred spirits," I say.

He looks sideways at me again. "No. I already have a kindred spirit. I'm your pal, Louisa. When you were a baby and I walked into the room, your eyes lit up. Just seeing me!"

This makes me smile. I remember when I was four years old I had a temper tantrum. My parents sent me upstairs to "think about it."

Jake came upstairs and into my room. "That was a good tantrum," he said. "And you were right to have it. We learn a lot from suffering a bit afterward."

I never forgot that. Jake is right. We were pals even then.

"Where's Boots?"

"She went shopping with her friend Talking Tillie. I don't have much time for my project."

"Project? What project?"

He looks at me. "Come on, Louisa. Hurry and eat up."

He hurries out the screen door, letting it slap behind him.

Project?

I pick up a piece of toast and share it with Tess. I take two quick bites. The rest will wait for me.

And we both go out the door.

There is early-morning sun, but no Jake.

"Jake?" I call.

"In here," he calls back.

I see the garage door is open. Tess and I walk over and look inside.

Jake is pushing a soft rag over the gleaming black car.

And standing next to the car is a boy a bit taller than I am.

His hair is the black color of Jake's car. His skin is brown.

We stare at each other.

Jake looks up.

"This is Louisiana. Louisa, this is my friend George."

Tess goes over to George and he bends down to pat her. Then he straightens up.

I open my mouth, but nothing comes out.

George has no idea what I am actually thinking and can't say to him.

Jake looks at George, then at me.

"Louisiana is probably thinking that you are pretty swell."

George smiles.

I can feel myself blush. I am startled.

Jake knows.

"Then I'll admit I have never seen anyone with the beautiful red color of your tumbling hair," says George.

Tumbling hair?

I can't help smiling back at George.

"Even steven," I say.

"Even steven," George repeats.

"Okay," says Jake loudly. "Now that we all like each other, get in the car! Boots will be back in an hour. We can only do this when Boots is gone. She wouldn't approve of us driving when we drive on the road."

"Where are we going?" I ask.

"This is my project," says Jake. "Get in. I'm teaching George how to drive my car."

Jake opens the back door of his beautiful car. I get in. Tess surprises me by jumping in beside me.

She's done this before.

Jake sits on the passenger side, not the driver's side.

George gets in the driver's seat, starts the car, and backs out of the garage, down the driveway, and onto the road.

"Still no seat belts," I say from the back seat.

George looks at me in the rearview mirror. I can tell he's amused.

"No seat belts," says Jake. "This is a 1938 car. Same age as I am."

We drive up the road.

"Is George allowed to drive on the road?" I ask.

"Not legally!" says Jake cheerfully.

Then we avoid one of the neighbors' chickens

running down the road. We turn and go up into the land behind Jake's house.

Beside me, Tess wags her tail and looks out the window, leaving dog nose marks there.

We drive around the field and the pond, George working the clutch and brake smoothly.

A heron flies up from the pond, then flies back again.

When we return home, down off the grass hill and onto the road, we go back to the garage.

George grins at me.

"Even steven," he says, holding up his hand.

I put my hand against his.

His hand is cool.

"Even steven," I say.

We are friends.

3

The Mirror

After George leaves, Jake and I walk back to the house.

"Boots doesn't know George and I drive the car when she's away," says Jake.

"You think?" I ask.

"She wouldn't approve," says Jake. "Don't tell her."

"I don't know if I can do that, Jake."

"You can try," says Jake.

I remember saying to Boots that I could *try* to stop change.

"George is your kindred spirit," I say.

Jake smiles. "He is."

"And Boots is your soul mate," says Jake.

I reach over to hold his hand. "And you are my pal," I say.

"And here is my secret. Boots doesn't know that I plan to give George the car. He loves it the way I do."

"But what about Boots driving?"

"She would never drive that car. She only drove once, and never again. And she knows nothing about gears and clutches."

Jake and I go into the kitchen where Theo is drinking orange juice, his eyes bleary from sleep.

Suddenly I stop and look at myself in the mirror hung by the door. I look at my long mop of red hair. I stare at the look of me.

"What's Lou doing?" asks Theo.

Jake turns and comes over to stand behind me as we both see ourselves in the mirror.

"Louisa is, I believe, thinking of herself as beautiful for the first time ever," he says.

"She's always been beautiful," says Theo.

"Not as beautiful as today," my pal Jake says to me in the mirror.

I am not looking at me, actually.

I'm looking at my "tumbling" red hair.

Boots comes home with Talking Tillie. They carry bags in. We all go out to help, Tillie talking about the sky this morning, the rain in the middle of the night, "and my cat who caught three—three, count them!—mice in the night and left them on the rug for me to step on in the morning."

When Talking Tillie is gone, Theo and I put away the groceries. Jake goes out to the garage.

"I'm going up to pick a new book to read," says Theo.

"How many books did you bring?" I ask.

"Forty-eight," says Theo, bounding up the stairs.

Boots laughs.

"What's new?" asks Boots, peering at me.

I shrug.

"George was here," I say lightly.

"Aha," she says. "And did Jake and George drive on the road and up around the pond?"

"You know about that?"

Boots looks closely at me.

"Oh, right. You know everything," I say.

"I do. Plus, Jake never realizes that the hood of his car is warm when he's been off driving with George."

"You're sneaky, Boots."

"I am."

"I went too," I confess. "And Tess. When he can't see to drive anymore, maybe you can drive," I say to Boots.

"Not me. Not Jake's car. He loves the car as much as he loves me. I'm not about to change now."

"But, Boots, you're the one who told me that change could be exciting. An adventure!"

Boots stares at me.

"Gotcha," I say.

"Gotcha," says Boots in a low voice.

She leans back in her chair and stares at me.

I thought about saying "even steven" to George and George saying "even steven" back to me with our hands together.

I was quiet. Boots was quiet.

I didn't tell Boots that George loved my "tumbling" hair.

I didn't say I thought George was beautiful.

"Did you drive a car when you were young, or did Jake drive when you met him?" I ask.

Boots smiles. "Jake and I met in middle school.

We fell in love across the classroom. Doing home-work together. Walking home after school, laughing all the way. I was thirteen when I fell in love. How old are you?"

"Almost twelve," I say.

"Imagine that," says Boots. "Falling in love at your age."

I say nothing.

"And you never drove a car?" I ask.

"Once I did. But not Jake's car. And Jake would never have the patience to teach me."

I grin.

"But George would," I say in a low voice.

Boots doesn't say anything for a long time.

Theo comes back to the kitchen with an armful of books. He drops them on the table, sorting them into piles of "yes, I'll read now" and "later."

I think about Boots and Jake falling in love so young.

No one I ever heard of fell in love at age twelve.

So here is the question of the day: Why, when I look in the mirror now, do I suddenly look beauti-ful for the very first time in my life? Is it a mistake somehow? A strange moment that will slip away like clouds?

I walk over to the mirror and look at myself.

My heart skips a beat.

I am beautiful.

4

Walking with George

In the middle of the night I get out of bed and go downstairs for a drink of water.

Boots is there, sitting in the half dark. She doesn't look up when I fill a glass.

I wonder if she's thinking about George teaching her how to drive Jake's car.

I'm thinking about George too.

I sleep late into the morning, and when I start to go downstairs, there is George, as if my thoughts called him to our house.

He's sitting across the table from Boots.

Theo is there too. He is showing George a few of the forty-eight books he brought to the island. George picks up one of Theo's books.

"I love *Julie of the Wolves*," says George. He picks up another book. "*The Devil's Storybook*, too. I have a copy of *Tuck Everlasting* I'll lend you. I have many books at home in my library."

"You have a library?!" asks Theo, excited.

George nods. "I call it my library," he says. "Upstairs, outside my bedroom, I have four bookshelves, floor to ceiling. And a chair with a footstool."

Theo's eyes grow wider.

"You can visit anytime. I even have overdue books there from the island library."

This makes me smile.

On the table is a basket of large tomatoes.

George looks up at me standing on the stairs.

"Mermaid girl," he says.

Boots smiles.

George's mother sent us tomatoes from her garden.

"She is overrun with them," says George. "She plants and forgets.

"She's an editor," says George to me. "Sometimes she writes poetry of her own. I call her One Word a Week Willa."

Boots laughs.

George stands up.

"Would you come to dinner at my house tonight, Louisa?"

"Me?" I say, surprised.

"You," he says with his amused look.

"Can I come too?" asks Theo.

George shakes his head. "Not this time, Theo. Just Louisa. The two of us. Like a date."

Theo opens his mouth, surprised. He looks at Boots.

Boots looks at me.

A date? I've never had a date. I'm not old enough.

"Sure," I say after a moment.

I realize I've only said two words—"Me?" and "Sure."

Theo and Boots look back at George.

There is a lot of head turning here.

"I'll come to walk you to my house at six o'clock," he says. "And I'll walk you back home. It's not far."

"Okay," I say.

Another single word!

George goes to the door, then turns.

"Don't change your hair," he says to me.

And then he goes out the screen door. Tess goes over to watch him walk away.

Theo looks at me. Boots does not.

I go to the refrigerator and open the door. "Do we have any orange juice?" I ask.

No one speaks. When I turn they are both smiling.

"It is not a date," I say firmly. "George and I are friends. Friends," I say more firmly.

They keep smiling.

"Why is Louisa dressed up?" asks Jake when I come downstairs at six. "Where is Theo?"

"I sent him to feed the sheep," says Boots.

I give Boots a grateful look.

"I thought I already did that," says Jake, looking confused.

"I'm going to dinner at George's house," I say.

"Oh," says Jake, no longer confused. "Nice."

Tess goes to the door and wags her tail.

George is there.

I go out the door. Tess whines behind me.

George doesn't say hello.

"Can you walk a mile, Louisiana?" he asks.

"I can. And I will."

George looks over to the sheep field and sees Theo staring at us.

"Your fault," I say. "You told him this was a date."

"I was amusing myself," says George.

Talking Tillie drives toward us on the dusty road, slows down to look at us, then waves. We wave back.

"Now our secret is out," I say.

George and I both burst out laughing. We laugh because we both know this is not a date.

We pass through the small town center.

George points. "That's my school," he says.

"That's a house!" I say. "My school is a large brick building with lots of classrooms and a large lunch-room where we line up for lunch."

"Poor you," says George.

I stare at him.

"We eat in a large dining room, all ages, young to older. Parents make wonderful lunches in the kitchen, and we all serve each other. Sometimes *we* cook too."

"It sounds like a home," I say.

"It *is* a home," he says simply. "Sometimes the older children help the younger ones. I'm helping some with reading."

I told Boots I hate change. But George makes change sound more interesting to me.

"You're confusing," I tell George.

"I know, Louisiana."

We stop walking.

"What?" I ask briskly.

"This is my house," says George.

"Oh."

"And Tess has followed us," he adds.

I turn and see Tess wagging her tail.

We both burst out laughing again.

Like friends.

5

Hands

George's house sits on a hill above the water. It has weathered shingles with a porch all around. It looks like a house in a book.

Tess runs up the steps in front of us.

"It's fine. Tess visits us often. My mother and father like her. When we tell her it's time to go home, she goes."

We open the door, and George's father, very tall and darker than George, smiles at me.

"Louisiana with the beautiful hair," he exclaims. "I'm Eliasi," he says, holding out his hand.

I take it. It is warm. And I do not feel shy.

"Don't tease her," calls George's mother from the

kitchen. When she comes into the room, we both stare at each other and smile.

Her hair is wild and curly, just like mine. She has tied it back, but not successfully. Curls pop around her face.

"Hello, Louisa. I'm Willa," she says. "And hello, Tess. What would Tess like to eat?"

"Toast," George and I say at the same time.

"Eliasi is the cook, but we can make toast," says Willa as I follow her into the kitchen. "I made . . . "

"Caprese salad!" I exclaim. "My favorite! No one in my family makes a beautiful salad like this!"

There is a huge platter of large sliced red tomatoes and basil leaves and thick slices of mozzarella cheese drizzled with oil and vinegar.

"Yay," says Willa.

"Yay," I repeat.

"I am grilling fish," says Eliasi. "Unless you don't like it, Louisa."

"I like it really, really crisp," I say, feeling brave to say so.

Eliasi smiles his huge smile. "I shall burn the fish for you, Louisiana."

And he does.

I eat three pieces of Eliasi's burned fish. And half the caprese salad.

Tess sleeps under the table by my feet.

"Willa and I met in Tanzania," says Eliasi. "She was working with the women and children in the villages. I fell in love with her hair before I fell in love with her."

"Boots and Jake fell in love across the classroom in middle school," I say. "Very young."

George is quiet, listening to our talk.

"I would have fallen in love with Willa if I'd met her in school," Eliasi says quietly. "It happens."

The sun has set. Tess has eaten crisp toast made by George.

"I loved your fish," I say to Eliasi.

"I love you for loving it," he says.

"And I loved the salad."

Willa smiles.

"As Jake would say," says George, "now that we all like each other, let's get going home."

I laugh.

And then I surprise myself.

"I'd like to come again."

Eliasi reaches over and holds my hand. "Of course."

"Of course," echoes Willa. "There will always be tomatoes."

"That's for sure," says Eliasi.

We wake Tess and say good-bye and start home again.

"Kwaheri!" Eliasi calls from the porch.

"That means 'good-bye' in Swahili," says George.

"How do I say 'thank you' in Swahili?" I ask.

"Asante," says George.

"Asante!" I call, and see Eliasi smile.

"He will teach you more Swahili," he says. "He likes you."

It is late dusk with a low red line of sunset on the water.

"Your mother has hair like mine," I say.

"You noticed," says George with a grin. "My parents married in Africa. And I was born there. This was my mother's island home. My father loved it because it reminded him of living by Lake Tanganyika, in Africa, where he fished."

"What does he do?" I ask.

"My father went to school to become a teacher," George says. "He teaches African studies at a college on the mainland. Sometimes he teaches at my school. And he still fishes."

We walk all the way home without more words, watching Tess sniffing the smells of the road, and the grasses, and the sea.

"Asante," I say to George when we get to the house.

George reaches over suddenly to put his hand against my hair—only for a moment.

I think of Eliasi's large, comforting hand.

George hadn't said hello when he came for me.

And he doesn't say good-bye.

I put my hand up to my hair where George's hand had been and watch him walk home again.

He turns once to look at me, walking backward. Then he is gone.

When I go inside, Boots and Jake are alone in the kitchen, dancing close together. There are candles on the table, flickering light in the dim room. Jake puts his hands on either side of Boots's face as they dance.

There is no music.

Hands again.

They don't notice me.

I walk past them and up the stairs to my room.

Hands.

"Louisa?"

It is night, Boots whispering in the dark.

"Yes?" I lift my head off the pillow.

"I didn't see you come in tonight."

"You were dancing with Jake," I whisper.

I can imagine Boots smiling at this.

"Did you have a good time at dinner?"

"Willa made caprese salad," I say, half asleep. Boots leans over to kiss my head.

"See you in the morning."

I don't remember her leaving.

6

Pretending

When I get up in the morning I walk by Theo's bedroom. His door is closed.

I am surprised to see the wall clock says it is only seven.

I look outside. Boots is walking across the driveway to the garage. She looks like she is walking carefully so she won't make noise in the gravel. The garage door is open.

I go outside and follow her.

She stands just inside the open door, looking at Jake's car.

When she sees me, she puts her hand out to stop me. She puts a finger to her lips.

George is inside the car, sitting quietly, his hands on the shiny steering wheel.

After a moment she takes my hand, and we back out of the garage.

George never sees us.

"I didn't want George to see us and feel shy. He often comes here early, before he and Jake drive off," she whispers. "Sometimes in the evening, as if to say good night to the car."

"Good morning and good night," I say softly.

We walk into Boots's flower garden outside the kitchen door. There are gravel paths and plants spread around, their colors contrasting and mingling like paints in a paint box.

There are asters, dahlias, red and yellow irises, and trillium. And flowers I don't know.

I point to a lacy bush. "What is that?"

"Astilbe," says Boots. "My favorite."

A sea breeze comes up and ripples the astilbe blooms.

Boots has already cut a large basket of blooms.

"So, did George tell you that I called him and asked him if he'd teach me to drive Jake's car?" asks Boots.

"No!"

Boots nods. "I figured he'd keep it to himself."

"What did George say?"

Boots smiles. "He said 'I don't think I can do that.'"

Boots picks up the big basket of flowers.

Her face is nearly hidden by blooms.

"But there are a few things I know," Boots tells me. "Jake wants to give his car to George when he can't drive any longer," says Boots. "He told me that last night. George has helped Jake for years. Since George was just a young boy."

I remember Boots and Jake dancing in the kitchen.

"I wonder why I didn't know George when we were younger, all those summers," I say.

"George and his parents spent summers in Africa back then." Boots smiles at me. "And maybe this was the best time for you to meet George," she says.

I don't answer her.

"And what is the second thing you know?" I ask.

"George loves that car," says Boots. "Which leads me to the third thing I know. I'm happy. I don't have to drive Jake's car. And I'm hatching a plan."

"What plan is that?"

"You'll know when I know it," says Boots.

She hands me the basket of flowers to carry into the kitchen.

"Let's go inside so George can pretend he just arrived to drive with Jake."

Which we do. George comes into the kitchen a few moments later.

"Flower maidens," he says. "What are you doing with all of these flowers?"

"Some will go to the clinic," says Boots. "Some will go to the library. And some will go to Willa."

Jake comes into the room, a little startled to see us all. He gives us a quick, thoughtful look, then goes over to Boots. He puts his arms around her and kisses her for a long, long time. I don't know if I've ever seen such a long kiss. Boots begins laughing with their lips together.

"My mother and father do that pretty often," George says. "Do your parents do that?"

"My parents are scientific researchers," I say. "They don't kiss in front of us."

Both Jake and Boots laugh now.

Then Theo, standing on the stairs, announces, "My friend Joey says my parents have kissed two times—once for Louisa and once for me," he says.

Jake and Boots laugh even harder.

George smiles at me. I smile back.

I'm not sure what we are all smiling about, but there is one more truth about me that no one knows.

I'm good at pretending that I know what I don't know.

7

Remembering a Face

Jake sits at the kitchen table, staring at a booklet and his medicine bottle.

I see that Boots's rubber wellies by the back door are gone. Tess is gone. They must be walking.

Jake doesn't look up and smile as he usually does.

I sit next to him.

A booklet is open to a page with a grid of lines.

I look at the booklet title: *Macular Degeneration*.

I feel cold all of a sudden. I never heard the name of what Jake had. Somehow giving it a name makes it more scary.

"I can't read my medicine bottle today," Jake says

without looking at me. "The test grid is more wavy. I called my retinal doctor on the mainland. He's going to see me today. There is a new treatment."

Jake gets up and goes to the mirror by the door. The mirror I've looked in so many times. He stands there.

"With macular degeneration you lose the central part of your retina sight. The middle of what you see," says Jake.

He pauses.

"I'm remembering my face," he says. "While I still can."

I go over and put my arms around him. "I know your face," I say. "If you can't see it, I'll tell you about it."

Jake turns into the old Jake then, hugging me. "My pal," he says.

And then Boots comes in, taking off her wellies, wet from the ocean or the dew of the meadow. Tess goes over to her water bowl and drinks and drinks.

Life seems the same as it is every day.

But not for Jake.

I look at Boots, and she reads my mind.

"We'll be gone for the day," she says. "Eliasi is

driving us to the boat this morning. We'll be back on the late boat, and we'll walk to Eliasi's house. Jake will have drops in his eyes and can't drive. Eliasi will drive us home again. Okay?"

"Okay."

But things are not okay, and Boots knows I know it. I know what is really on Jake's mind. He will lose the middle of what he sees when he drives.

Not seeing the road is worse for Jake than not seeing his face.

Eliasi arrives a bit early in his gray pickup truck with a surprise. Sitting between George and Eliasi is a big smooth-coated brown dog. When he opens his door, the dog leaps over George and jumps down from the truck. Tess is more than happy, leaping around with the brown dog.

"We have a dog!" says George.

Eliasi gets out. "I found him in my boat yesterday. He went fishing with me. He's my sea dog."

George looks at me, knowing what I'm thinking. "He isn't owned by anyone on the island," he says. "We called the dog officer. The ferry driver said he gets on the boat and rides to the island. He stays for a few days. Then he reappears and takes the trip to the mainland again. They keep food and water for him on the ferry."

"He's my sea dog," repeats Eliasi. "I call him Rafiki."

"What does 'Rafiki' mean?" I ask.

George holds up his hand. "'Friend,'" he says.

Theo comes out of the house with Boots and Jake. Rafiki runs to them.

New friends!

"Come for dinner tonight," Eliasi calls to us all. "It's dance night!"

"I don't dance," I say.

"I don't dance either," says George. "My parents dance all the time. Even when there's no music."

"Dancing is easy," says Theo. "I've watched. I'll show you later. I have art class this afternoon at the school."

"Micha?" asks George. "You'll like her. She teaches art during the school year. She tried to help me paint a tree."

"How did it go?" I ask.

He shakes his head. "My tree never looked alive," he says.

"That's fine if the tree is lying dead on the ground," says Theo, trying to be kind.

Boots and Jake laugh.

"I'll try to remember that I am good at painting dead trees," says George.

"And don't worry about dancing," adds Theo. "Dancing is just two people, looking bored, hanging on to each other and moving around."

"Boots and I dance," says Jake. "And we're never bored."

"Never," says Boots.

Then Rafiki and Tess run off to the sheep field, sending the sheep running.

Jake and Boots get up in the truck.

And they are gone. Driving down the road to ride the ferry to Jake's eye appointment.

I watch.

"Let's walk with the dogs," says George to me. "It'll take your mind off of Jake's eyes."

"You're getting more like Jake every day. Knowing what I'm thinking," I say.

"Maybe," says George. "Or maybe it's easy to see what you're thinking. Your face tells me."

We are quiet, ducking between the rails of

the fence and walking through the field.

The sheep look up, then away again.

The morning is cool, the sun not yet summer hot.

We can see Tess and Rafiki down the sandy beach, noses to the sand, smelling scents the seals have left behind.

"What would you do if you were losing your eyesight?" I ask George.

He thinks for a moment. "I'd memorize the world," he says. "Remember it."

I stop walking. "That's what Jake said this morning," I say.

George nods. "I'm turning into Jake," he says. "You said so."

"George!" A small boy waves from down the beach. He begins running.

"Marco!" shouts George. "Marco goes to school with me."

Tess and Rafiki run with Marco. They reach us in a heap of dogs and boy.

"This is my friend, Louisiana," says George. "This is Marco."

"Louisiana is a state in the South," says Marco.

"It is," I say. "I was named after it."

"I read about it," says Marco. "George taught me how to read! I read every night. I think about you every night," he says to George.

"I think about *you* every night too," says George.

"I'll think about you thinking about me," says Marco.

"And I'll think about *you* thinking about me," says George.

We all laugh and walk together. Suddenly Marco runs ahead and picks something up from what a sea wave left.

He hands me a small moon snail shell, rounded and perfect and wet from the water.

"For you, Louisiana," says Marco.

"Thank you, Marco," I say. "I'll put it next to my bed. And now I will think about you every night too."

Marco smiles at me.

"Marco!"

Marco turns.

"My father and I are spending the day together," he says, beginning to run down the beach. "We're going to the library!"

Marco runs to his father. He turns to wave at us once.

George stands very still and watches Marco.

"You taught him to read?" I say.

George nods. "My teacher Maggie asked me to help him one day. 'Marco likes you,' she said. 'You can help him.'"

A wave comes in.

"And now Marco is teaching his father, Angelo, to read English," he says so softly I hardly hear him. "They're going to the library."

"And you did that," I say.

"I began it," George says.

I hold up my hand. "Rafiki," I say. The moon snail shell is under my thumb.

George takes my hand and holds it, the shell between our hands. "Rafiki," he says.

And he walks up through the meadow and home.

8

Eyes

It is dance night at George's house. Eliasi has strung tiny white lights along the porch roof and railings and into the house, even though it isn't yet dark.

George and I walk up the porch steps, Theo catching up with us.

"How was the art class?" asks George. "Did you like Micha?"

"I did," says Theo. "She said I am a 'thoughtful' painter."

"Really? What did you paint?" I ask.

"I don't know," says Theo. "But it was thoughtful."

George laughs.

"My friend Dahlia painted big bright things. Dahlia is a kind of wild girl," Theo says.

George nods. "I know Dahlia."

"Marco is very precise," says Theo. "He did many lines that ended up as a face! We're going to begin a project together."

A project. That word I remember hearing from Jake.

"Don't ask me about the project," warns Theo, holding up his hands as a shield. "It is presently a secret."

I am fairly sure the word "presently" is Micha's word.

"I have hamburgers and salads, cheeses, pickles, and chips," says Eliasi, coming out on the porch.

"Could I eat later?" asks Theo. "I want to see George's library."

George points to the stairs just inside the door.

"What about *samaki*?" I ask Eliasi slyly.

George had told me the Swahili word for "fish."

"And burned *samaki* for Louisiana!" says Eliasi, looking impressed. "Come in, come in, and then after dinner we'll dance."

"Not me," I say softly.

"Not me," whispers George.

Inside Willa is wearing a long black dress. She has sparkling stars clipped in her curly hair. They catch the light as she moves.

"Louisa! I have something for you, for later. Do you have a pocket?" asks Willa.

"Yes. What is it?"

"I'll show you when we dance," says Willa.

Willa hands me a small cloth bag. I put it in my pocket. And then I see the huge caprese salad on the table.

I grin.

George laughs. "Even I am beginning to like it."

"You go ahead and eat," says Willa. "Eliasi and I will wait for Boots and Jake. It won't be long."

Willa goes to the kitchen, and we see Eliasi suddenly take her in his arms, the two of them dancing slowly across the room.

"See?" says George. "No music."

I nod. "I saw Boots and Jake dance without music."

George and I eat. George even eats burned *samaki*.

I can't stop watching Willa and Eliasi, dancing and turning around the kitchen together.

"It isn't about the music, is it?" I say.

"No," says George.

"And it isn't really about the dancing, either."

I stop eating and put down my fork. I fold my hands under my chin and lean on the table, looking at George.

He puts down his fork, folding his hands under his chin, leaning on the table, imitating me.

"What are you two doing?" asks Theo, sitting down in front of the large hamburger Eliasi has left on his plate.

"We are speaking to each other wordlessly," says George.

"Oh," says Theo. "Is it working?"

"Yes," says George.

"Yes," I say.

No one speaks for a moment.

"I want a library," says Theo finally, almost mournfully.

"I'll help you," says George.

"You will?"

"I will," says George, nodding. "We have extra bookshelves in the cellar."

Theo sits back and stares at George for such a

long time I think Theo might be about to cry. Some-times Theo does that, cries after thinking for a long time about something sad or something for which he is grateful or excited. But instead, Theo looks at the kitchen as Eliasi swings Willa out and then back in his arms.

"They don't have music," he says, making George smile at me.

"And they're kissing now," Theo adds.

And they are.

George shakes his head.

"It's not about the dance," he says again.

I can't think of anything to say.

And then the loud ferry horn sounds. The ferry is coming into the small harbor.

Rafiki and Tess come out from under the table, Rafiki's ears up, listening.

The horn sounds again.

We all walk out to the porch, Rafiki running down the steps.

"Rafiki!" I call.

"Let him go," says Eliasi. "Maybe he'll get on the ferry. Maybe he'll stay. He has his own life. But he'll come back when he wants, I know."

"Like my parents," I say.

I could be having an exotic life somewhere with them.

Eliasi puts his arm around me. "Like your parents," he repeats.

I look up at Eliasi. "How do you know Rafiki will come back?"

"He likes my burned *samaki*," says Eliasi.

"And he *loves* my father," says George.

"Like your parents," says Eliasi.

The sun is setting. Dusk will come soon.

"I hope Jake is all right," I say.

"You can worry about Jake's eyes," says Eliasi very softly. "But you never have to worry about Jake."

I can feel tears in the corners of my eyes. I brush them away.

"Louisiana?" says Eliasi.

"What?"

"Look," says George.

I look down the hill. And there are Boots and Jake walking up, Rafiki running ahead of them, leading the way.

"We're back! I got a shot in the eye!" calls Jake. "Let's dance!"

It is nearly dark and the tiny white lights seem brighter now. Boots and Jake sit at the table to eat before they dance.

Jake sees me watching him. He holds out his hand and pulls me closer.

"I had a little 'leakage' in my eye, Louisa. The doctor gave me a shot to clear it up. My eye will see better after a while."

And then the music comes on, slow and sweet. Theo comes downstairs from the library.

Willa pulls me to the mirror. She takes the little bag out of my pocket. It is filled with star clips. She clips them all around my terrible hair, so that soon, in front of my eyes, I look enchanted.

I say that to Willa.

"We're all a little enchanted," she says.

"Come out to the porch where no one will watch you," calls Theo. "You have to be a beginner before you can dance like Willa and Eliasi. Just remember to look bored."

"I'm not sure about this," calls George from the kitchen.

"Me neither," I call to him.

George comes out of the kitchen and stops when he sees me. "What have you done?"

"Willa did it."

George keeps staring at me. "You sparkle," he says finally.

I shrug. "It's dance night," I say.

Rafiki comes out from under the table with a dill pickle hanging out of his mouth, while Tess sleeps.

George and I laugh.

Dance night.

So here is my startling story about dance night.

It is dark on the porch, but the music and white lights make it pleasant and that word "enchanted."

"Bored, remember," says Theo.

But as it turns out it is Theo who is bored in the end. He watches as George puts his hand on my waist and takes my hand. And somehow we know how to dance, as if we had been taught long ago in another life but had forgotten until now.

We have never been this close to each other before. Even our eyes are close. I see Theo leave the porch and go up the stairs to George's library.

I think about eyes—Jake's eyes, better for a while.

George turns us around and we move closer.

"Are you bored?" asks George, his mouth close to my ear.

"I don't feel bored," I say.

I can feel George sigh against me.

"I'm not bored at all," he says.

And then I look into George's eyes. I can see the reflection of the stars in my hair there.

Eyes.

I can see George—

And I can see me.

Eyes.

9

The Library

George and Eliasi come the next morning, with two large bookcases in the back of the truck and Rafiki in the front. They carry the bookcases to the large upstairs hallway outside Theo's room.

Theo has that old look like he might cry. Surprisingly, George leans over and hugs him.

"I'll help you carry your books out," says George.

George and I look at each other shyly, remembering our dancing closely the night before.

Eliasi notices. "You two did very well dancing. The emphasis is on the word 'very.'"

Jake, bringing out a lamp to put by the bookcases, smiles.

"Very," Jake repeats.

George looks at me. I duck my head and don't look at him.

"I found a chair we're not using," says Boots, pushing an easy chair out of her bedroom and down the hallway. I help her carry it over by the bookcases and lamp.

"That's your favorite lamp," says Boots to Jake.

"I don't use that lamp anymore," says Jake. "I'm passing in on to Theo."

There is a sudden silence.

"I don't," says Jake. "Get to work."

And we do. And soon the books are on the shelves.

"Oh, I forgot," says Jake suddenly. He disappears into his room and comes out with a picture.

He has a hammer and a nail. He pounds in the nail and hangs a picture. It is a picture of Jake, sitting and reading, his favorite lamp behind him.

"I took that picture," says Boots. "Remember?"

"No," says Jake. "I don't remember. I was reading!"

Boots laughs.

Suddenly Rafiki bounds up the stairs, happy to discover all of us. He jumps into the chair and watches us.

Theo stands very still and looks at the bookshelves, filled with his books, the lamp, and the chair for a moment. Then Theo moves Rafiki over a bit and sits on his chair. He strokes Rafiki's head.

"My library," he says. Then softer, "My library."

He doesn't cry.

"That was a good thing you did for Theo," I say in the kitchen.

"I understand him. I like Theo," says George.

"I like him too."

"I know," says George.

I am about to make an intelligent remark about all the things George appears to know when he surprises me.

"Do you know that Theo wants to live here on the island instead of going home?" he asks softly.

"I know, but he can't, just like I can't go traveling with my parents."

All of a sudden the house is filled with people. Marco and Dahlia come into the kitchen. Jake, Boots, and Eliasi come downstairs.

"A party," says Jake.

"Hi, Jake. Where's Theo?" asks Dahlia.

Marco and Dahlia are carrying large rolled-up canvases.

"Upstairs in his library," I tell her.

"He has a library?!" says Dahlia.

Marco and Dahlia drop the rolled-up canvases on the kitchen table. They run upstairs.

"No party," says Jake, making us laugh.

Eliasi picks up Dahlia's canvas. Very carefully he unrolls it.

"Dahlia did this. It's me," he adds, though we all know it.

I catch my breath. It is a bold Dahlia-like painting of Eliasi. He is looking straight at us with a serious, thoughtful look.

"That's beautiful," I say. "I guess that means you are beautiful too," I add.

Eliasi puts his arm around me.

"Nakupenda," says Eliasi to me.

George grins. "It means 'I love you.' Or 'I like you,' either way."

"No, actually, you can say I 'like' a tablecloth. But when you say it to a person, it is love," says Eliasi.

Marco, Dahlia, and Theo come downstairs. Rafiki is behind them, trying to be first.

Tess barks at the screen door and comes in. She and Rafiki drink water noisily.

"Your painting of Eliasi is so good," I say to Dahlia.

"Thank you. Oh, I forgot to tell you that Micha is bringing Georgia by to ask you a question."

Marco unrolls his painting and holds it up.

Angelo's smile is the same as Marco's. His strong hands are on a fishing net that surrounds him like an ocean. He's not smiling at the painter. He is smiling at his work.

"Angelo," says Boots.

There is a knock at the door. Micha comes in with another woman.

"Is this a party?" Micha asks.

"I hope so," says Jake.

"This is my English teacher," says George. "This is Theo and Louisiana. Louisiana, meet Georgia."

Everyone laughs, even me.

"I think that is the first time I've ever laughed about my name," I say.

"Born in Louisiana?" asks Georgia.

"I was. And you?"

"What do you think?!" says Georgia.

We laugh again.

"I'm going to paint," says Theo.

"Could I paint?" asks Jake.

"You used to paint," says Boots. "When we first met. You painted my dog Jack."

"Just before he bit me," says Jake, remembering.

George and I look at each other. I know we are thinking the same thing—how can Jake paint when he can't see clearly?

"Anyone and everyone can paint!" says Micha.

"I came to ask George and Louisiana a favor," says Georgia. "We're going to paint some people on the island and hang the pictures in the library. The children in Micha's art class want to call the exhibit 'Secrets of the Island.' I teach George and know he is a great writer, and he says you have great insight, Louisiana. Could you two visit these islanders and write about them? To go with the paintings?"

I stare at George. How did he know that my words were private, inside my head? How did he know they were even there?

He sees my stare.

"Louisa is thinking that she only thinks interior thoughts. And she thinks in what I call 'spurts.'"

Spurts? That doesn't have a very intelligent sound to it.

"Ah, like a poem, maybe?" says Georgia. "A poem is fine too."

"I will help with the interviews," says George, "but Louisa should be the writer. She has unique observations."

"I can think of interesting people to visit: Billie the bird woman, Ashley the writer, artist, and puppet maker . . ."

"And Angelo and Eliasi," adds Micha.

"Good. I think we should do this every year—the islanders will get to know each other in new ways," says Georgia.

And then they are gone. And George is going to make me pull out my private thoughts and put them on paper.

George smiles at me.

I don't smile back.

10

Words

"Are you still mad at me for getting you into this?" asks George as we walk to our first interview.

"Yes," I say.

George smiles, not at me but to himself, which makes me doubt everything—whether I can write, whether I am really mad.

"She is," echoes Theo, who is walking next to me.

Theo has asked to come with us.

"I've read all of Ashley's books," says Theo.

We walk on.

"There's Ashley's house," says George.

I am quiet, and George looks over to me.

"You're scared, aren't you?"

Now I really hate George because he knows.

Ashley's house looks out over the water.

ASHLEY

George knocks on the door.

"Come in!"

We open the door and walk into a room filled with toys and paintings, and puppets almost as tall as Theo.

"I'm out here," calls Ashley.

He's in his painting room, and he turns and smiles.

His face is the same color as George's face.

"Welcome to my world. I was born far away, and when I came to visit the island one day I knew I wanted to live here forever."

"Yes!" says Theo fervently.

"You too?" asks Ashley.

He peers closely at Theo.

"You too?" he repeats in a kind, understanding voice.

Theo nods.

"I'm Theo," my brother blurts out as if he can't help it. "I've read all your books."

"Then you deserve a look at the book I'm working on now," says Ashley.

"George has told me you are his best friend, Louisiana. *Loo ees ee anna.*" He sings my name. "Beautiful name."

He stretches out his words.

His voice is music. I feel the way Theo sometimes feels—tears in my eyes, moved by Ashley's interest and understanding of Theo.

And his kindness.

When we say good-bye to Ashley, Theo walks backward, still looking at Ashley's house.

"You're very quiet," says George.

I take a deep breath. "I'm writing in my head," I say. "I can do this."

"I know you can," says George.

"We could begin the piece 'His voice is music,'" I say.

I put out my hand without looking at George, and he takes it.

We walk down the road, holding hands.

Theo still walks backward.

George and I, Theo, Dahlia, and Marco all traipse up the hill to visit Billie. Dahlia has brought her large sketchbook.

"She's a friend of my mother's," says Dahlia. "I want to draw her so I can paint her with a bird and more."

"A bird and more?" I ask.

"You'll see," says Dahlia with a strange, happy look.

Dahlia doesn't knock at the front door. She beckons us around the house. There are many trees. I can hear a fountain in the backyard.

And then there is Billie in a chair, with birds everywhere—at her feet, on the chair, on the ground around her, on the low limbs of trees.

Billie, slim with hair less red than mine, waves a hand at Dahlia. When we walk into the yard, a cloud of birds flies up in a tree, peering at us. But one stays.

"This is Louisa and Theo," says Dahlia. "You know George and Marco."

"I do. Hi there." She points. "This is Kiki, the mother of many of those looking at you suspiciously. Do you want to feed her?"

Billie pours some birdseed into my hand. "Just hold out your hand. She's a chickadee. They're very tame."

I am startled when Kiki flies to my hand. I feel her tiny feet on my palm. I hold my breath as she stays there for a moment, then flies away with a seed.

Billie smiles at the look on my face.

"Can I do it?" asks Theo.

"Sure. Here's some seed."

"The birds have always come here." Three flock to Theo's hand. His eyes widen at the feel of them.

"Here come the titmice, Marco. They're more timid, but they're beautiful in the hand with their big black eyes."

"I can see the eye," says Marco. "My father says crows are very smart."

"Angelo is right," says Billie. "They come from time to time. They left my mother and father gifts when they fed them. And I have a basket full of them. They're on the table."

The other birds fly down, and Billie feeds them.

In the basket are shells, many beads, a child's red barrette.

"The birds and I are kind to one another," says Billie.

And then there is a huge cloud of birds around us all.

And as Marco holds out his hand, a cardinal comes, picks up a seed, and flies up to the tree.

"Ah, a treat for you, Marco," says Billie.

Marco doesn't say anything, but stares up at the tree, looking at the cardinal.

Even though there are dozens and dozens of birds fluttering and cheeping around us, this seems to me one of the most peaceful and calm places I've ever been.

We walk home. George looks at me.

"First line for today?"

"A bird and more," I say. "Those were Dahlia's words."

"You are good at this."

"I know."

11

Nakupenda

Boots is in the kitchen early. Theo is sleeping.

"Where's Jake?"

"That is a mystery. He's shut himself in the study. I think he's painting."

"What's he painting?" I ask.

"That's about the one thing I don't know," says Boots.

Suddenly I lean over and kiss Boots.

"What's this?" she asks.

"I like you."

"No, you *love* me," says Boots.

George knocks and comes into the kitchen. "Jake called and said he was busy today," he says.

"He's painting," I say.

"The car," we say together.

"My father is lending me the boat today. Want to go out? It's sunny. We'll take Rafiki. We don't have more interviews until tomorrow."

Boots looks at me. She gives a quick, almost unseen nod. I run upstairs and put on my bathing suit.

When I come down again, Boots hands me a towel and her beach bag. And when George and I leave the house and I look back, Boots is standing at the door looking after us.

Rafiki jumps into the boat, happy to be going somewhere. We motor out. There are white clouds in a blue sky.

The ferry is going out to the mainland. There is a sudden pang in my stomach as I watch it, thinking of the end of summer, of going back to school, of leaving the island.

George drops the anchor and sits next to me on the bench.

We don't say anything. We've had a week of words, of interviews.

And then Rafiki jumps off the boat into the water.

I stand up.

"Can he swim?!" I call to George.

"I've never seen that."

I run to the stern of the boat and jump in. "Rafiki?"

George begins to laugh. Rafiki is swimming around me. Suddenly, I feel a cramp in my leg. I try to tread water, but I can't.

"What's wrong, Louisa?"

"A cramp in my leg."

George takes off his shirt and dives into the water beside me. He holds me up.

"All right, Louisa?" he asks, holding on to me.

We are very close together, his face close to mine.

"I think so," I say.

We look at each other.

And then George kisses me.

Then he leans back.

"What is this?" he asks.

"I don't know," I whisper. "But you can do it again."

And he does.

Our bodies are as close as friends can be.

And to make him feel better, I kiss him back. And

we begin to laugh, our lips together, like Jake and Boots laughing while they kiss.

Rafiki paddles over to nose us, making us laugh more.

"Is this *nakupenda*?" asks George suddenly.

There is shock on his face that he has said it.

"Like a tablecloth?" I joke, echoing Eliasi's words about "like" and "love."

"No," says George. "Not like a tablecloth."

I burst out laughing and he laughs more.

And then, because we don't know what to say, we climb back up on the boat and help Rafiki up.

Rafiki shakes water off his coat.

A cool breeze makes me shiver. I dry myself with my towel and hand it to George. We don't say anything the whole way back to shore except for once.

"Your curls shine from the sea, Louisiana," says George.

Nakupenda.

When I walk into the kitchen, Boots is alone.

"Where's Theo?"

"Off with Dahlia and Marco."

"Where's Jake?"

"Still in the study, doing whatever he's doing."

I sit down at the kitchen table.

"George kissed me," I say in the stillness of the room.

"Of course he did," says Boots.

I stare at Boots.

"I kissed him back," I say as if it is a confession.

Boots smiles. "Of course you did."

I stare at her, a sudden sense of relief coming over me like a soft blanket.

"Jake and I were in sixth grade when we kissed each other for the first time," says Boots. She pauses for a moment.

"It was a sweet beginning," she adds softly.

I stare at her across the table.

"Theo, Dahlia, and Marco will be here soon. You might want to get into dry clothes."

I nod. I walk to the stairs and go halfway up, then turn.

Boots still smiles at her own memories.

Theo, Dahlia, and Marco come clattering into the kitchen, carrying their paintings. I am startled to see George with them.

We look at each other, then away.

Dahlia unrolls her painting of Billie.

Billie with her muted red hair, her figure soft—several birds at her feet and a titmouse in her hand, with its large staring black iridescent eye.

"Billie will love this painting," says Boots.

Jake comes into the kitchen carrying a large canvas. He peers at the painting.

"You'll grow up to be a fine painter," he tells her.

He looks at us all.

"I have a painting of my own," he says.

He looks embarrassed. I have never ever seen Jake look embarrassed.

"The car?" George and I say together for the second time.

Jake looks at us, amused.

"More important than the car," he says.

Jake turns the canvas around.

I am stunned.

It is a painting, hazy, but it is clear to me that it is Boots. You can't tell her age by the painting. It is almost Boots at all ages, like an impressionist painting. Boots young and older.

No one says a thing.

"I wanted to paint Boots as I saw her then and see her now, before my eyes get worse," says Jake, almost apologetically.

Jake peers at me.

"That bad?" he asks.

"That perfect," I say.

"And much more important than your car," says George.

"Yes," says Theo.

"You're a painter too," says Dahlia.

"Only a painter of Boots," says Jake.

"I look perfectly beautiful in this painting," says Boots.

"You *are* perfectly beautiful," Jake says. "And you were beautiful the day I first kissed you in the eighth grade."

"Sixth," says Boots, laughing.

George and I look at each other shyly. Theo notices.

"What's up with you two?" he asks.

George shrugs. I shrug.

Theo turns away.

12

Language of the Island

In the night I find Theo sitting on the top step of the stairs.

"Are you sick?" I ask.

Theo shakes his head. In the moonlight I can see tears at the corners of his eyes. I sit next to him and put my arm around him.

"I don't want to go home at the end of summer. I want to stay here," says Theo.

"I don't think we can do that."

"Why not?" Theo asks me.

He turns to look at me.

"Why not?" he says again.

I sigh. "You know, once Boots told me sometimes

something happens to make things right," I tell him.

"What?"

"Sometimes things happen. Like the moon rising at night and the sun in the morning. And things happen to change the things you don't like."

"There's not much of the summer left," says Theo. "That 'something' better happen soon."

"Go back to bed. You can think about it in bed."

Theo gets up and goes to his bedroom door. He turns. "Maybe that 'something' is me," he says.

"Good night, Theo."

"Good night, Louisa."

Maybe he's right.

ELIASI

Eliasi sits at his kitchen table, his long legs stretched out. Rafiki nuzzles his hand for pats all through our talk.

"I look very serious and thoughtful in my painting. And that is just the way I am."

"You are not," says George, laughing. "You smile all the time."

"Stay out of my interview," says Eliasi with his

great smile. "I was very serious until I met and fell in love with Willa."

"Do you like it on this island?" asks Theo.

"Living here gives me great joy. It reminds me of where I lived in Tanzania. But there it was a very big lake, Lake Tanganyika, the second deepest lake in the world. I could look across the lake and see the Congo. Here it is the sea, and I look across and see the mainland."

Eliasi thinks a moment. "I love looking over water," he says.

I write that down. George watches me do it.

Walking over to Angelo's fishing boat, George taps my shoulder.

"So, 'I love looking over water' is your first line?"

"Or *your* first line," I say to George. "Georgia called you the great writer."

"We all know who the real writer is," says George. "Hmm, or maybe the last line."

"Good point," I say.

"There's my father!" says Marco.

Angelo waves at us from his big fishing boat, tied up at the wharf.

ANGELO

We jump onto Angelo's boat, named *Bianca*.

"Why is your boat named *Bianca*?" asks Dahlia.

"This is my home away from home. It is Marco's mother's name. I like to bring my wonderful wife with me while I fish," says Angelo.

"Did you live on the island when you were a little boy?" asks Theo.

I thought of Theo on the stairs last night, wanting to be a boy living on the island.

"I came here when I was young," says Angelo. "I should have learned to read English better, but I spent lots of time fishing with my father. Now that Marco is teaching me, I spend lots of time in the library when I'm not fishing."

"I have a library at Jake and Boots's house," says Theo happily. "You can come see it anytime and borrow books."

"Thank you, Theo. You know something I've learned through all the seasons—summers and winters and storms? I've learned that the island has a language all its own. And I know that language well."

George and I look at each other and write in our notebooks.

Herring gulls fly over the boat, calling out, then flying on over the stretch of water. A cloud covers the sun, and it is shaded and then bright again as the cloud passes.

Part of the language of the island.

I look over at Theo and I know he is thinking the same thing.

13

"That Blue"

Boots had gone shopping with Talking Tillie. She had been off with Talking Tillie on errands many times, sometimes not even coming home with groceries. *What is she doing?* Jake was gone somewhere too.

This time it was Theo who disappeared into the painting room, as Jake now called the study. Theo had said nothing about what he was doing.

George and I sit down to write together at the kitchen table. George is quiet. I think he is embarrassed that he used the Swahili word for love. I decide to get it over with.

"Now that you love me, we should have no trouble writing well together," I say to him.

He stares at me, then bursts out laughing.

"All right, all right. I love you, Louisiana," he says.

Now *I* am embarrassed.

"You don't have to say that," I say.

"I know. But . . ." He pauses. "It's true."

Neither of us know what to do. Finally George picks up a pen and hands it to me. "Write."

ASHLEY
His voice is music.
He sings his words
in a world of color
and shapes—
puppets who dance
joyfully.

BILLIE
A bird and more
come to her
sit in her hand
with their fragile feet.
"The birds and I
are kind to
one another."

ELIASI
"Living here gives me great joy."
From Lake Tanganyika
to this island.
"I love looking over water."

ANGELO
Through all the seasons—
hot summer winds,
cold,
and storms—
this "island has a language all its own."

George and I work together, talking about words and other words and changes and whether to use commas or dashes.

Then we are done and are silent again.

Finally I pick up the pen and hand it to George just the way he had handed the pen to me before we began.

"Done," he says.

"Yep."

"It's pretty fine."

"The people we interviewed are pretty fine," I say.

And then the door to the "painting room" opens and Theo comes out, carrying a large canvas. He has paint smudges on his face, making him look much younger than he is.

He walks over to us, saying nothing. He turns the canvas around.

"Jake!" exclaims George.

It is a painting of Jake with the most surprising blue of Jake's eyes looking out at us.

"Jake will love this," I say to Theo.

George wipes a smudge of paint from my cheek.

There is a slap of the screen door and it is Jake. He stares at the painting. He is quiet for a moment.

"I will remember this painting clearly, even when I can't see well," he says to Theo. "That's the great thing about memory. And it is the great thing about this painting."

I start thinking about what to write for Jake's work of art.

A car stops outside.

"Yikes," says Jake, who does not tolerate Talking Tillie well. "I'll just wait until Boots sees Theo's painting. Boots will cry. You just watch. Then I'll go upstairs and read a book while Talking Tillie carries the rest of the groceries inside while talking too much."

"You can't read, Jake," says Theo.

"Oh, right," says Jake, making us smile.

But Boots comes in alone, carrying two grocery bags. Tillie's car drives away.

"Where are the rest of the groceries?" asks Jake.

"This is all today," says Boots. "I had a secret errand."

"What?" asks Jake.

"Secret," Boots repeats.

She puts the bread away, then the cheese and meat in the refrigerator.

"You got a tattoo!" jokes Theo.

"That's it, Theo," says Boots.

And then Boots sees Theo's picture of Jake. She stares for a minute. Her eyes widen, then fill with tears.

"See?" says Jake, putting his arms around Boots.

"Theo did that picture," I say to Boots.

Boots cries more.

"That blue," says Boots, crying. *"That blue."*

"Okay, Boots," says Jake. "I'm going upstairs to read a book now."

"You can't read!" says Boots, wiping her eyes.

And we all laugh. Even Boots.

But I know why Boots is crying.

That blue.

14

This Is Great!

It is almost the end of summer. You can feel fall in the air. I know it, and I am sure Theo knows it too. The paintings are all framed and will be hung in the library soon.

"Jake's and Boots's paintings will go up in two weeks," I say.

"But that's almost the end of summer," says Theo.

We finish dinner late, and it is dark outside. After we help with the dishes, Boots goes off to bed. Theo and I start upstairs to our rooms.

The phone rings, and for some reason it makes me jump. Theo and I are at the top of the stairs, his library light glowing in the corner.

"Hello," says Jake. "Well, hello—where are you?"

Theo and I know. We know it is our parents calling.

"What exciting news is that? Oh, okay. We'll look for you then."

Jake turns and looks at us at the top of the stairs.

"No, sorry. They've gone to bed. But I'll tell them you called."

Jake hangs up the phone. "I lied," he says.

I smile. "You're forgiven," I tell him.

"They're coming on the weekend—just passing through. They say they have exciting news," says Jake. "You know what I know."

"Good night, Jake."

"Good night," he says.

Theo looks at me and goes to his bedroom door.

"Good night, Louisa," says Theo. "I have to do something."

"What kind of something?"

"I don't know," says Theo, looking as sad as I've ever seen him.

He opens his door and goes inside, shutting the door behind him.

What something?

I am surprised by my next thought.

I hope his something works.

In the morning we find out a bad storm is coming. It is dark and rainy, with strong wind gusts. George, dripping with rain, comes to see if he can help us. He takes off his raincoat and hat by the door.

"My father and I took our boat out of the water and helped Angelo secure his. My mother is bringing in all of her potted plants and cutting some flowers to bring in."

"We should do that," says Boots.

"Rafiki won't go outside," says George.

"Dogs know," says Jake. "Want to go outside, Tess?"

Tess looks up, yawns, and closes her eyes again.

"What about the sheep?" asks Theo. "What if there is lightning and high winds?"

"Good question," says Jake. "I never fixed the barn roof. It's too dangerous for them."

"Maybe you can take the car out of the garage and put the sheep in there," says Boots.

We all looked at Jake.

Jake turns to look at Boots, his mouth open as if he is about to say something.

Boots bursts out laughing.

"Come on, old fellow, you know we're going to bring them into the kitchen! Remember, we once had seventeen hens and a rooster in here during a hurricane."

"I remember," says Jake. "The rooster pecked at the shells of my poached eggs. George, maybe you could help me bring in the fencing. We can put the sheep in the corner with hay and water."

"What about our parents coming here?" asks Theo.

"They're not coming until after the storm passes, if the ferry is running," says Jake.

"It's not running for a few days," says George.

"Okay. I have time to think," says Theo.

"Think about what?" asks Boots.

"The 'something' that sometimes happens," says Theo.

"Oh, *that* something," says Boots.

The wind grows stronger. Boots and I cut lots of flowers and bring them in. We carry in pots of flowers.

There is thunder and some lightning.

George and Jake bring in fencing to the corner of the big kitchen. They carry in hay, and Theo spreads it around the floor. And then the wind grows stronger and some of the trees bend down. We go out to lead the sheep, Bitty and Flossie and Flip, into the kitchen.

They are peaceful, even staring calmly at Tess through the fence.

"This is great!" says Theo.

And the lights go out. We find candles and oil lamps.

George goes to the phone to see if it works. He dials.

"Hi. I'm going to stay overnight to help out at Jake and Boots's house."

"Yes, her too," he says, looking at me.

Right after George's call the phone stops working.

"I have my cell phone," says George, "if we need it. My father said there may be some hurricane-force winds for the next day or two."

Boots has made spaghetti sauce already, and she cooks the spaghetti on the gas stove, which works without electricity. She has a roast in the oven for the next two days.

We eat by lantern light, the sheep starting to smell like wet sheep in a warm house.

"I should check the garage," says Jake suddenly.

"I did," says George.

"This is great!" repeats Theo.

"It is," says Boots.

"It is," says Jake.

"It is," says George.

They look at me.

"This is great," I say, grinning at them all.

Bitty looks at me and bleats loudly.

This is great.

15

The Storm

In the night the winds grow worse. We can hear small branches falling on the roof. The sheep lie down happily. George sleeps on an extra mattress on the floor in Theo's room. I can hear them talking when I get up for a drink of water.

George comes out of Theo's bedroom and sees me on the top stair.

"George?" I whisper, tapping his shoulder.

"Yes?" he says, tapping my shoulder back.

"You told Eliasi about kissing me, didn't you?"

"Yes, and you kissing me back," he adds.

"And what did he say?"

"He nodded the way he nods when I tell him I'll mow the lawn."

"Maybe he didn't hear you."

"He heard me."

"I told Boots you kissed me," I say.

"And what did Boots say?"

"She said 'of course he did.'"

"That's the same thing as my father nodding at me," says George.

"I suppose so," I say.

"I know so," says George, sounding a lot like Boots.

We can hear Jake downstairs talking soothingly to the sheep, though the sheep seem peaceful.

I touch George's shoulder. "Good night," I say.

George touches my shoulder back. "Good night, Louisiana."

All night long the wind blows hard. I sleep and wake, sleep and wake. When it is morning the storm is still fierce and I hear the bleating of the sheep downstairs. George is sitting at the kitchen table watching Jake cook breakfast.

The sheep have been given bowls of breakfast too.

"The sheep love apples," says George, watching me come down the stairs.

"Is Theo still sleeping?" I ask.

"He is. I woke up in the middle of the night several times and Theo was sitting up in bed, thinking."

"Yes. Theo is thinking about how to figure out the rest of his life."

"Aren't we all," says Jake, bringing three plates of poached eggs on toast to the table.

He looks at us. "Aren't we all?"

George and I look sideways at each other, George raising a questioning eyebrow at me.

I shake my head. No, Boots had not told Jake we kissed. Boots keeps secrets. My mind goes back to the first time I met George, in the garage, by the beautiful black car. Jake had known my thoughts about George then. Maybe he knew our secret now. Sometimes I think the worse Jake's eyes become, the more things he knows. Like paying attention to things only Jake sees in his head. Once he told me what Helen Keller said about blindness—"the only thing worse than being blind is having sight but no vision."

Bitty and Flossie begin bleating again as the wind blows and the rain pounds against the windows.

The storm goes on, hail pellets beginning to hit the windows now.

"Jake?" says George.

"What?"

"Teach me?"

"Teach you what?"

"How to make your poached eggs."

Jake smiles. "My pleasure. Louisa is right. You are turning into me. It's an art of butter and timing."

"And it is *my* pleasure being you," says George.

I shake my head. "Soon I'll be outnumbered," I say.

"No," says Boots at the kitchen door. "You've got me."

"I do!"

Theo comes down the stairs. "Who have *I* got?" he asks.

"Us," says George. "And Jake's great poached eggs. And *what* do you have as well?" adds George. "You have a library of books with words you will carry with you all of your life."

Everyone looks at George. He is amused at our looks.

"That was very intelligent, wasn't it?" he says.

"Yep," says Jake, handing George the box of eggs. "You are me."

"Then *who* am I?" says Theo, his voice rising.

All of the sheep—Bitty and Flossie and Flip—look at Theo and begin to bleat loudly. *"Baa, Baa. BAA."*

We all laugh.

The kitchen is filled with the noise of people and sheep.

George cooks four poached eggs on toast and gives the sheep more apple slices. He tosses crisp toast to Tess. Then Theo and Jake shovel out the old hay into buckets, put on their rain gear and boots to get fresh hay and check the barn and trees.

Boots watches them out the window.

"This is a long storm," she says. "It's still rough out there. I haven't opened the freezer so we'll have food for days."

I sit down at the table. "I kind of like it," I say.

"I do too," says Boots. "We all get to take care of each other inside, even the girls."

I smile that she calls the sheep "girls."

"My parents called," I say.

"I heard that. I heard they are 'passing through,'" says Boots. "It's not yet the end of summer."

"I'm going to tell you a secret," I say.

"Okay."

"Theo doesn't want to go home. He told George. He told me. He loves it here."

"I know that," says Boots.

"I forgot . . . ," I begin.

"That I know everything," finishes Boots. She shrugs. "Something will happen," she says.

"That's what Theo is waiting for."

"It will happen," says Boots. "I know that because . . ." She waves her hand.

"You know everything."

That night, when everyone has gone to bed, the sheep sleeping peacefully in their new hay, Jake and I go up the stairs together.

"Jake?" I whisper.

I seemed to be whispering in the dark these nights.

Jake turns to me. As always, Theo's lamp by his library shelves is on.

"Did Boots tell you anything about George and me?"

Jake smiles. "No. I know lots of things about you and George, but not from Boots. And all the things I know are good."

I nod.

Jake puts his arm around me.

"My pal," he says.

And we go to bed, waiting for the storm to end.

16

Silence

We had two days of storm, no electricity. Even George's cell phone didn't work anymore. We ate everything in the refrigerator and freezer as time went by.

Eliasi drives to our house to make sure we are fine.

"This should be the last bad day of the storm," he says, hugging Boots.

Tess is happy to see a new person. He pats her and she leans on him.

"I'm ready to get back outside with my car," says Jake.

"Louisa and I have liked it—with the people and

sheep inside," says Boots. "Would you like to take a sheep home?"

Eliasi laughs. "No, thank you, Boots. But you're right. It changes the nature of life on the island. We realize we are small when the weather comes."

"Want me to come home?" asks George.

Eliasi shakes his head. "No. Willa and I are having a lovely romantic time together."

"Dancing probably," says George.

"You betcha," says Eliasi. "You can be more help here, I think. There will be limbs to haul and some damages to barns and sheds."

"What about the ferry?" asks Theo.

"It will be ready to go day after tomorrow," says Eliasi. "Maybe," he adds.

I know Theo is thinking of our parents visiting for a day.

"The paintings are all hanging in the library, Micha told me," Eliasi says. "They knew the storm was coming and finished all the work early," said Eliasi.

Eliasi kisses George good-bye. He pauses, then leans down to kiss me good-bye too. Then he is out the door in the rain and wind.

"I have something to do if you don't need me," says Theo.

"What?" I ask.

"Something," says Theo, already going upstairs.

"Your fault, that 'something,'" I say to Boots.

"What are you talking about?" asks George.

"I'll explain it to you later," I say. "It kind of involves my meeting you in Jake's garage that first morning."

"I was right about that, wasn't I?" says Boots. "That 'something' was really 'something.'"

"Oh, *that* kind of something," says George.

Boots and I look at each other.

"Hey, how about I make poached eggs on toast for dinner," says George happily. "Then we can dance!"

"We'll have no music," I say.

George peers at me. "You know it isn't about the music, Louisiana," he says softly.

Boots doesn't say anything.

Jake doesn't say anything. But he takes Boots's hand and pulls her into the middle of the kitchen. They dance, the sheep watching them as they move, closer together. The sheep eyes follow them as they turn around and around.

"See?" says George.

George takes my hand and puts his arm around me, and we dance, turning around, his face close to mine.

"We'll have eggs later," George whispers in my ear, making me smile.

He pulls his face away from mine so I can see him smile too.

We don't know how long we dance, Jake and Boots, George and I. It could be minutes or longer. An hour maybe. George puts his hand on my cheek. I suddenly remember the day he first put his hand against my hair and how that changed me.

I move closer to him, our faces almost together. I think about kissing him.

Then he stops dancing.

"What?" I whisper.

He begins to dance again.

"Silence," he whispers.

And suddenly I know that George doesn't mean no music.

The storm is over. Only rain. No whining wind. No hail against the windows. Silence.

I kiss him.

Too fast for Boots and Jake to see.

17

The "Something"

We eat George's eggs for dinner, the four of us, Boots and Jake giving me smiles. I know they saw me kiss George as we danced. Theo falls asleep in his bedroom and sleeps all night. When I go upstairs I find a paper next to him on the bed.

It is about Jake.

JAKE
Our caretaker
The something I need
Who sees all
Without eyes

I stare at it. And I know what Theo is trying to do. He is writing down the "something" that will help him keep us on the island instead of going home.

I leave quietly.

The morning is clear and quiet. It seems odd, all the silence.

George and Jake go outside to check on damage and downed trees.

Boots is feeding the girls in the kitchen.

"We'll lead them back out to their field when George and Jake check the fences."

I nod, still thinking about Theo's words.

"What's wrong?" asks Boots.

The phone rings.

Boots answers it.

"Hello?" I know.

"Hi, Millie. Yes, we had quite a storm. No electricity or phone for a few days."

There is a pause.

"Today? Is the ferry running?" Another pause.

"Hi, Jack. You should know it is a mess here, trees

down. We have the sheep in the kitchen. Okay, then. Here and gone again? See you."

Boots puts down the phone.

Theo comes down the stairs. "They're coming today?" he asks.

"Just for a while," says Boots.

A car drives up outside, and Micha knocks at the door.

"Come in, Micha," calls Boots.

"Sheep in the kitchen during the storm? What fun!"

Bitty bleats at Micha.

She bends down and pets them all.

"I came to get the writing to go with Theo's wonderful painting," she said. "We're going to put it up today."

Theo walks down the stairs and hands his paper to her.

"But you're the writer, Louisa," he says to me.

"Your 'something' speaks for me," I say. "Use Theo's words."

"Lovely," says Micha. "May I take this?"

We both nod.

"We'll put up Boots's painting next week. Who is writing about her?"

I look at Boots. "I wanted to write about Boots, but Jake might want to."

Boots shakes her head. "I know what Jake will say. He'll say, 'My painting is my thoughts of Boots.'"

Micha laughs.

"Well, you've got time, Louisa," says Micha.

Jake and George come in the house.

"Jake, can Louisa write the words that go with your painting?" asks Boots.

"Or do you want to do it?" I ask.

"No," says Jake. "My painting shows how I feel about Boots. You write what you know of her, Louisa."

Micha smiles at Boots. She goes out the door and gets into her car, still smiling at us through the car window.

Theo and I look at each other.

Our parents are coming.

Jake and George are out mending the sheep fence when my parents arrive in the late afternoon.

My mother comes in the door, looking very tan with her brown hair swinging around her.

I hug her, not sure of how happy I am to see her.

Theo gives her a kiss. My father comes in, sees the sheep in their kitchen pen, and laughs.

"Island life!" he says.

He hugs Boots, then Theo, then me.

He is wearing worn brown boots.

"You've grown up this summer," he says to me.

"I have."

"Where's Jake?"

"Mending the sheep fences," says Boots.

I look outside and see a car with a driver waiting.

"I'll go get him. I want to share our news with him. We can't stay long this time."

My father goes out the door and down to the sheep fence. I can see him and Jake hugging. I see him shake hands with George. I feel like I am watching a performance onstage.

They walk back to the house and inside.

"This is George, my friend. My mother."

"Hello, George," says my mother with a smile.

"I'm glad to meet you," he says.

"Why is the town driver here?" asks Jake.

"We're going back as soon as the ferry leaves again," says my father. "I'm sorry for a quick trip this time."

"We have great news for all of us," says my mother happily. "Jack has a grant for at least two years to travel and study in many exciting places. We'll take you with us, and you can go to school wherever we stop! Isn't that wonderful? I've already spoken to your school."

There is a silence.

Theo has a look of great relief on his face, as if a path has opened in front of him. I know he has something to say, but I can't figure out what.

"That is wonderful for you," Theo says. "And I'm glad you spoke to our school. Louisa and I have been very involved with projects on the island, and they will take at least one year, maybe two."

I see George smile at the word "two," given to Theo by my mother.

"I . . ." Theo looks at me. "Louisa and I want to stay here and go to school and continue our island project."

There is a greater silence now. My mother doesn't speak. My father is silent, staring at Theo.

"I can travel back and forth to my music lessons, so that won't change. I'll go back and forth on the ferry with Rafiki," Theo says.

He smiles at George.

"Who's Rafiki?" asks my mother, looking stricken.

"My dog," says George kindly.

And my mother begins to cry.

"Would anyone like a cup of tea?" asks Boots.

This makes George smile again.

"I love it here," says Theo simply. "It is my home away from home. And," he adds softly, "I have a library here. A library!" he repeats.

"But we love you!" my mother cries out.

"And we love you. But I love Boots and Jake, too. And they love us. And I have good friends here."

"But you'll be a wanderer, back and forth on the ferry," says my mother, tears still on her face.

"No," I say suddenly. "*You* and Dad are the wanderers. We want to stay in the place we love with the family we love. With friends and teachers who care about us. And with projects that are important to us. Like yours are to you."

My words startle me.

Jake clears his throat and looks at Millie and Jack. "You two have lived very independent and creative lives. Your children have learned very well from you."

"You can be proud of them," says Boots.

It is quiet.

Then our father surprises us.

"You're right!" he says. "I *am* proud of them! And we can't take them away from their work here."

He looks both happy and sad at the same time.

I go to my mother and hug her.

"This is right for us, do you see?" I say.

She smiles at me. She is quiet for a moment. "I do see," she says. "I do."

"I'm so glad you understand," I say to my father.

"It was what you said about *us* being the wanderers," he says softly. "And Theo, as young as he is, being so compelling. Your mother," he adds, "will understand as soon as she realizes that you have her strong opinions."

"I love you," I say.

"Me too."

"Would you and Mother like to see my library?" ask Theo in a poignant voice. "George made it for me."

Surprisingly, my mother goes over to George and hugs him. "That was a great thing to do for Theo. He's a great reader," she says.

"I was glad to do it," says George. "I love Theo. And I love Louisa," he adds.

My mother nods. "Love is good," she says, startling me.

She and George look at each other as if they shared something unspoken.

"Of course we want to see your library," says my father. He takes a breath. "But first I have something to do."

He goes outside. My mother comes over and stands next to me. We can see my father talking to the town driver, who is waiting there. After a moment the driver drives off.

"I think we're staying a night or two," she says softly, putting her arm around me. "Okay, Boots?"

"Very okay," says Boots.

When I turn to look at my mother, it is a bit like looking at myself—a version of me. Or I am a version of her.

My father comes back inside. "Now for the library," he says to Theo.

Theo leads the way as my father and my mother go upstairs, and it is quiet in the kitchen.

"Well, what about that?" says Jake.

"'Something' always happens," says Boots with a lilt in her voice, looking satisfied with herself.

The next day my father helps George, Theo, and Jake fix the barn roof and cut up fallen trees. My mother and Boots put out the pots of flowers and cook two or three days of food. My mother weeds the garden with great energy. And we take two long walks through the sheep field and down by the sea, Tess running ahead.

George comes for dinner the night before they leave.

"What birds do you remember from Tanzania?" asks my father.

George puts down his fork.

"A few. The malachite kingfishers are colorful with bright orange bills. My father says this bird is more beautiful than any jewel. And then . . ." George stops to think. My parents have already put down *their* forks, captivated by George.

Theo and I smile at each other.

"And then there is the lilac-breasted roller, who flies in a rolling fashion, not in a straight line. And"— George gathers steam—"there is the very large shoebill stork, a three-foot-tall bird that has binocular vision."

He looks at my father.

"You know that is rare in birds," my father says.

All of the rest of us are staring at George.

"The Ross's turaco with scarlet wings. And some of the yellow weaver birds, which make interesting woven nests with entry tubes that hang down. And my mother's favorite birds, the little fire finches. That's about all I remember."

George stops talking then. He looks around the table.

"Nobody's eating," he says.

"We were busy listening," says my mother with a great smile.

"I'll say," says my father with admiration.

We all pick up our forks and eat again.

My mother and father steal admiring looks at George.

When it is dark, George and I go outside. I hold up my hand next to George's.

"Rafiki," says George.

"Rafiki," I say.

"I just remembered another bird," he says.

I grin.

"Save it for next time."

He reaches over and puts two fingers on my lips.

And I watch him walk home under the moon.

My mother and father go to bed early since they have to catch the first ferry to the mainland.

At the top of the stairs I put my arms around Theo.

"You were the 'something,'" I tell him.

"Actually, Mother and Father were the 'something'—planning to travel, talking to our school."

Jake and Boots come upstairs then.

I turn to them suddenly. "Did we ever ask if we could stay?"

"In many ways," says Jake.

"In *all* possible ways," says Boots simply.

18

A Dream Within a Dream

In the morning Theo and I kiss our mother and father good-bye for now. We watch them drive away to the ferry.

So, this is close to the end of my life story so far that began with anguish—when I hated change.

I've been given courage by an eight-year-old brother who is brave.

And Jake and Boots, who are thoughtful caretakers.

And parents who may be "dense," as Boots once put it, but who know us better than we thought. They are brave.

And my friend George, who when we first met

held up his hand and said, "Even steven."

Boots tells me I could like George and love George at the same time. So I will like him and kiss him every so often.

I can be brave too.

Today, sadly, the sheep have gone back to their green field. Tess has gone out too, so she can tell them where to go and where not to go. They will, of course, ignore her.

Boots has gone off on some kind of secret venture.

Theo went back to sleep.

I sweep up the last bits of hay on the kitchen floor.

I wipe the table of breakfast crumbs.

I wash the poached egg pan and smile that George made poached eggs for us all.

He was inventive.

"This is good. What's this?" asked Jake, happily poking at something with his fork.

George shrugged. "I found it in the refrigerator."

"Buttered asparagus with a touch of lemon," said Boots with a smile.

"But I hate asparagus!" said Jake with a shocked look. "It's good I'm half blind. At least I can't see it."

And he went on eating.

So I wait.

George and Jake have gone off to admire the 1938 midnight-black Cord car.

The barn roof is finished.

There are no more tree limbs on the ground.

Theo runs down the stairs. "Louisa! Look outside!"

I hear shouts coming from outside. Jake and George.

Theo and I go out where Boots has come home.

She gets out of a green truck and pats it.

Boots driving a truck?

George is grinning, walking around the truck and looking it over.

Jake has no words.

Boots hugs him. "I learned to drive. I got my license!"

"Look!" she tells Jake, pointing at her boots. "My truck is the color of my wellies!"

> BOOTS
> *Truth teller*
> *her arms around me*
> *making the truth safe to know—*

calm comfort—
And a wellie-green truck
all her own.

My life is a dream within a dream.

31901064828967